The Other Kitten

Books by Patricia M. St. John

Friska, My Friend

The Other Kitten

PATRICIA ST. JOHN

The Other Kitten

BETHANY HOUSE PUBLISHERS
MINNEAPOLIS, MINNESOTA 55438

Published by Bethany House Publishers
A Ministry of Bethany Fellowship, Inc.
6820 Auto Club Road, Minneapolis, Minnesota 55438

Printed in the United States of America

ISBN 1–55661–152–8

1

When Mark first woke, he lay there, still half asleep, trying to remember. Then he woke properly and it all came back to him. He jumped out of bed, ran to the window, flung it wide open and stuck his head far out.

What a morning! The sun was just rising behind the trees at the bottom of the garden and the dew on the grass sparkled like silver, except for the golden patches where the daffodils grew. The birds were singing wildly, madly. Mark dressed quickly and opened his suitcase to see that nothing had been forgotten. He pushed aside the clothes that Mom had packed and checked the really important things: his roller skates, his parka, his swimming trunks (he was determined to swim, even though Grandma said it was too cold), his underwater goggles, snorkel and cricket ball. His bat and shrimping net would be strapped to the case and he would carry his football under his arm. Everything was in order.

He thought he had better wake Carol in case she made them late, fussing over her packing. He crossed to her room where she lay asleep, her hair spread all over the pillow, pulled the bed sheets off her and tweaked her toes. She sat up, started to be upset, and then remembered too.

"It's today, isn't it?" she said.

"Of course, silly; you don't think it's yesterday, do you?"

She ran to the window. "It's a lovely day," she said. "I'm going to say goodbye to the rabbits."

Carol was so sure of her packing that she had strapped it all up the day before, with her bucket and shovel on top of the case. She pulled on her jeans and shirt and ran downstairs and into the garden. She picked some dandelion leaves as a farewell present and disappeared around the corner of the house. Mark was left alone.

"I'd better wake Mom and Dad," he thought. "We've got to get to Grandma's by lunchtime and they take a lot longer to dress than we do." He decided to take them a cup of tea and made it very carefully, warming the pot and pouring milk into the pitcher. When he reached the bedroom, carrying the tray, he kicked the door open with a bang. His parents both opened their eyes, blinked and yawned.

"What on earth do you think you're doing, Mark?" said Dad. "It's only a quarter past six."

Mark placed the tray on the bedside table. He poured out two cups of tea and sat down on the rug with his cup of juice. "You said you wanted to start early," he reminded them. "I was afraid you might oversleep."

"I didn't mean *this* early," grumbled Dad with another yawn, but they both sat up and drank their tea.

It was cozy and still half dark in the bedroom and Mark suddenly wondered if he

wanted to go away after all. "You'll tell us when the baby comes, won't you?" he said. "I hope it's a boy. Carol's hopeless at baseball."

Mom laughed. "It can't be long now," she said. "But Carol wants a girl, so someone is going to be disappointed. Dad and I have decided to be pleased with whatever comes. Anyhow, where is Carol?"

"Saying goodbye to the rabbits. Dad, you'd better get up, and you too, Mom. You take so long to dress. I'll put out breakfast and bring down the luggage."

Dad grumbled a little but decided that it would not hurt to start early. "The sooner we go, the sooner I'll be back," he remarked to Mom as he began shaving.

Mark had breakfast ready long before they had finished upstairs, but they appeared at last and Carol came in from the garden, sniffing and looking sad.

"I'll take good care of your rabbits, Carol," said Mom, "so don't worry. And there'll be wild rabbits in the field opposite Grandma's."

"And squirrels in the woods," said Dad.

"And lambs at the farm," said Carol, cheering up.

"And the old horse who sticks his head over the gate," said Mark. "I'm going to ride him this time. Mr. Cobbley said I could."

"And me," said Carol.

"No, you're too little. Mr. Cobbley said so."

"He didn't."

"He did."

"He didn't."

"Now, stop it!" said Mom. "If you argue like that at Grandma's, she'll pack you off home. Mark, you're the oldest; you must promise me . . ."

"Okay," said Mark. "I'll try; but it's Carol who starts it."

"I don't," said Carol.

"You do."

"I don't."

"STOP IT," said Dad so loudly that they both stopped at once. They stuffed their mouths with toast and marmalade and gave each other a kick under the table.

"Now let's be off," said Dad. "It was a good idea waking us so early, Mark. If we start at once we will be almost on the highway before the rush hour."

They hugged Mom and bundled into the back of the car, leaning out to wave and blow kisses. The streets were still quiet and the shops shut. In a very short time they had left the town behind and were out in the country where the fields were starred with daisies and the trees were bursting into leaf. And, although you could not hear them above the noise of the car, Carol knew that all the birds were singing as they built their nests. She stuck her head out of the window and laughed softly for joy. It was going to be a wonderful vacation.

2

It was a wonderful journey too, and they did not quarrel once. They played the animal game, seeing who could score a hundred first; one for a cow, one for a pig, two for a sheep or dog, three for a horse, and four for a cat. Carol even saw a rabbit, which counted for five.

Later, on the highway, they felt thirsty so they stopped at a service station and each had a can of soda-pop and an ice cream bar. They each had a turn on a Space Invader machine and then raced back to the car. The day was getting hot by now and the traffic was heavy. Mark was sorry when they turned off the main road because he loved racing the trucks, but Carol was glad. She loved the little narrow roads that wound up and down, and the glimpses from the hilltops of baby lambs in green fields. Then suddenly they both gave a shout for there was a sign ahead of them and it said DEVONSHIRE.

"Not long now," said Dad. "We'll soon see the tidal river, and then the sea."

The first glimpse of the sea was always exciting and today it was blue and tossing with little white waves breaking all over it. They turned south and soon the children began to remember the bridge across the river, the steep, steep hill to the cliff top and the wide coast road that climbed and dipped; then the cottages and the village shop, where they turned left into Grandma's lane. Two minutes more, and they caught sight of Grandma herself standing at the door to welcome them, and in thirty seconds they were out of the car and Carol had run right into her arms.

"Can I sleep in the little room where the roof comes down to the floor?" whispered Carol.

"Hello, Grandma," said Mark, pushing

Carol aside and giving Grandma a kiss. "Can we go to the sea this afternoon and can I swim?"

Grandma looked horrified. "In April?" she exclaimed. "I would think it is much too cold. What does Daddy say?"

"They're tough," said Dad. "Cold water won't hurt them. How are you, Mother? It's good to see you again."

They carried in the luggage and took it upstairs. Carol had the attic room where the roof came down to the floor, and Mark had the room overlooking the sea where he could watch the ships steaming up and down the Bristol Channel.

But they didn't have long to unpack because lunch was ready. They clattered downstairs to the low stone kitchen, where Grandma was serving up fried chicken and potatoes, followed by chocolate pudding.

Dad left soon after lunch and Grandma, who would not have minded a rest, got out her car, for the cliff road was long and steep. Mark and Carol flung their bathing things, snorkel, bucket and shovel into the back

seat. "Do we have to go in the car?" asked Mark. "Can't we run?"

"If you keep to the side of the road, you can," said Grandma. "But I'm not running, and you'll be glad for the car coming back. Now, off you go!"

They ran and ran, down through the dark woods where the stream ran along beside them below the road, and then out into the sunshine where the cottages began and great drifts of primroses grew on the banks. Grandma came behind them, parked the car, and ran with them down the rocky path that led to the beach. They had arrived, and the sun was shining, and small waves were breaking in foam on the sand.

"Quick," shouted Mark, flinging off his clothes. "Where's my snorkel?" He raced for the sea, but Carol was not in such a hurry. It was very cold and she did not stay in long. Instead she built an enormous sandcastle with Grandma, to try to stop the tide.

"How far does the water come?" asked Carol.

"Right up to the wall," said Grandma,

"and it's coming very fast. Look, there's hardly any sand left. We'll soon have to move the towels, and our castle isn't going to last long."

Mark came in from the sea to help. They shoveled more sand on the back of the castle and put stones in front, but it was no use. It soon crumbled and the sea seemed to be running up the shore. Everyone was packing up and leaving and the children were suddenly glad that they didn't have to walk up that steep hill. It had been a long, exciting day and by the time they had reached home and had some snack, and watched Blue Peter and visited the horse, they were quite tired. By seven o'clock, Carol's eyes were closing.

"You can't go to bed yet," said Mark. "It's much too early."

"It's the sea air," said Grandma, "and getting up so early. Suppose you have some supper now and then go up to bed, and I'll come and tell you a story."

"Oh, yes," said Carol. She loved Grandma's stories. Mark thought he was rather old for stories in bed, but he did not mind listening to Carol's. He gave a great yawn.

"Think I'll go to bed too," he said. "And I might come in and listen to Carol's story. Is it about smugglers and wreckers?"

Grandma laughed. "No," she said. "I'll tell you about them when we go to the wreck museum. Now, come and have your supper."

Half an hour later Carol had snuggled down in bed and Grandma was sitting beside her. Through the open attic window they could see the sky, still bright from the sunset. There was a wind blowing up from the sea and Carol wondered what it would be like on the beach with the dark waves breaking against the cliff. She gave a little shiver.

"Is it high tide now?" she asked.

"It will just have turned," answered Grandma. "There'll be plenty of sand tomorrow morning. Shall I tell you a story about a boat and a storm?"

There was a big bounce on the end of the bed as Mark arrived in his pajamas. "Me too," he said, curling up under the blanket.

So Grandma told them about a dark night, long ago, when the wind came sweeping down from the hills, whipping up the waves and the twelve friends of Jesus were caught in a storm as they tried to row across the lake. They thought their boat was going to sink, and they wished so much that Jesus was with them. But Jesus had stayed behind.

Then suddenly one of them looked up and saw someone coming toward them, walking on the water. At first they were very frightened and thought it was a ghost. Then they saw that it was Jesus coming to them.

"I've heard that story before," said Mark, "and I don't believe it. No one could walk on the water."

"Well, we couldn't," said Grandma. "But if Jesus was really God, then he made the sea and the land. And if you make something, you can do what you like with it."

"Be quiet now, Mark," said Carol. "Go on, Grandma, what happened?"

So Grandma went on. "Peter, one of the friends, saw Jesus and he thought, 'I'd rather be with Jesus on the sea than without him in the boat.' So he called out, 'If it's really you, tell me to come to you.'

" 'Come,' said Jesus, and Peter slipped over the side and he too walked on the water, looking hard at Jesus all the time. But suddenly he looked away and saw the great, black waves. He was very frightened and began to sink.

" 'Lord, save me,' he shouted.

"Jesus seized hold of his hand just in time. 'Why were you afraid?' he said. 'Why didn't you believe in me?'

"They walked back to the boat together. As soon as they got in, the wind stopped. Everything was safe and all right when Jesus was there. And it's still like that today," said Grandma. "If Jesus is with us, loving us and looking after us, then everything is safe and happy. But we have to ask him."

The sky was quite dark now, and two stars were shining in the window. Carol was nearly asleep. It had been a rather frightening story and she was glad it had ended like that, loved and safe and happy because Jesus was there. She thought of the wind and the waves and the high tide. She wanted always to feel safe and happy too. She would ask Grandma to tell her more about Jesus another night.

3

The next three days passed happily. They stayed on the beach when the sun shone, and if it was dull or rainy they went to the farm and fed a motherless lamb with a bottle. A little late lamb was born one morning and they watched it take its first wobbly steps. Every evening they phoned their mother to ask if the baby had arrived, but it seemed to be taking its time. However, they got news of the rabbits and told Mom and Dad what they were doing. The first night, they had a fight over the receiver and nearly pulled the phone onto the floor, so after that, Grandma stood by and timed them, one minute each.

And every night when Carol was tucked in bed, Grandma came and told her a story

from the Bible. Carol was beginning to think that the Bible was a very interesting book with so many stories about Jesus. He seemed such a kind person, always helping people and making them well and happy; and Grandma said that, although they could not see him, he was still there, ready to help anyone who asked him. Mark still said he did not believe it and he would rather have stories about wreckers and smugglers but he always came and listened, curled up at the bottom of the bed, and sometimes, when Grandma stopped, he told her to go on.

The time raced by, and it was not until the fourth day that they had their first real quarrel. They were just finishing breakfast;

Grandma was talking to the milkman and they were alone.

"I'm going to see the horse," said Mark. "Tell Grandma."

"You can't," said Carol, standing in front of the door. "It's your turn to dry the dishes. Grandma said we were to take turns."

"I did it yesterday," said Mark. "Get out of the way."

"You didn't," shouted Carol. "I did it at supper."

"Supper doesn't count. It's only a little bit. I did it at dinner so it's your turn."

"It's not!"

"It is!"

"Isn't, and I won't!"

"Neither will I. Get out of the way!"

"I will tell Grandma!"

"I don't care. Get out of the way or I'll push you!"

"You can't!"

"I can!" And he did. When Grandma came back, they were both on the floor, screaming and punching and scratching. Carol was smaller than Mark, but she could be very fierce.

Grandma could be quite fierce too. She pulled them apart and made them stand up. Carol was crying; Mark was sulking.

"He hit me on the head," sobbed Carol.

"And she bit me," growled Mark, showing the teeth marks on his arm. "She's a crybaby and it's her turn to dry."

"I'm not and it isn't!"

"You are and it is!"

"STOP IT," said Grandma. "I'm ashamed of you both. You can both dry and if there's any more of this you can stay apart in your rooms instead of going to the sea, and that would be a shame, because it's going to be a lovely day."

So they dried the dishes in angry silence, making faces at each other behind Grandma's back. When they had finished, she took a shopping basket and a list.

"Go down to the shop for me," she said, "and make up to each other on the way. It's the best day yet, and if you come back smiling and friendly, we'll go to Hartland Point this afternoon and see the lighthouse."

They set off, walking a long way apart but Grandma had been right. It was hard to remember a quarrel on such a bright day when everything was joyful. The birds were twittering excitedly over their nests and the lambs were skipping around their mothers. Mark ran to catch up to Carol and Carol stopped sniffing. By the time they reached the shop they were happy again and planning how to spend their pocket money.

There was only one shop in the village and they had to wait some time to be served. Mark stood in the line with the basket, but Carol wandered outside and looked around. There was a path behind the shop leading up to some cottages, and at the top of the hill was a trailer site. They had never been up there and Carol thought there would be a lovely view of the coast. Mark was sure to be ages; she would run a little way and see.

But she never got to the top of the hill, because when she reached the gate of the first cottage, she saw the sign. She thought it was the most exciting sign she had ever seen and she just stood staring and staring. This is what it said:

KITTENS GIVEN AWAY FREE TO GOOD HOMES

"Ours is a good home," thought Carol. A kitten was almost as much fun as a new baby. She must tell Mark at once. She ran back to the shop and found Mark, having finished his shopping, standing at the door looking for her. She grabbed his free hand.

"Come quick," she shouted. "I've found something lovely."

"What?"

"Come and see." She helped carry the basket and almost dragged him up the hill. When they reached the sign they both stood staring at it.

"Would Grandma let us?" asked Mark.

"She'd have to, if we took it back with us," said Carol. "Anyhow, we'd take it home soon. Mom wouldn't mind."

"I think we'd better ask her," said Mark slowly. He was determined to go to Hartland Point and he didn't want any more trouble.

"But, of course, we could always go in and look at them."

"Yes, let's," said Carol, pushing open the gate and dancing up the path. She knocked loudly at the door and a woman opened it.

"We've come to see the kittens," said Carol. "We've got a good home. We're staying with Mrs. White; she's our Grandma."

"Come in," said the woman. "They're ready to go, and I'll be glad to be rid of them. Your Grandma's a friend of mine; she'd know how to look after a kitten. They're all out here in the woodshed."

Mark and Carol knelt down in the woodshed and forgot all about everything. There were four kittens with long, soft fur and round blue eyes, crawling in and out of the basket or scampering back to their mother for a feed. Carol picked up a gray tabby; Mark picked up a black one with four white paws and a white nose.

"We'll take this one," he said, "and I will call it Tippet because of the white tips on its paws and nose."

"No," said Carol, "we're taking this one,

and I will call it Fluff because it's so soft."

"We're not," said Mark. "I'm the oldest so I ought to choose and I've made up my mind. I'll share it with you and you'll soon get to like it."

But Carol wanted the gray kitten more than anything else in the world.

"I saw it first!" she shouted. "I wish I'd come in to see them without you. We're taking this one, I say, or we're not having any at all."

The woman took away the kittens in a hurry. She was afraid the children might have a fight and pull them in half.

"Dear me!" she said. "I'm not giving you a kitten if you're going to quarrel over it like that. You can go back to your Grandma and ask her what she thinks. When you've made up your minds, tell her to come with you. I'll keep them until I hear from her."

She led the children out into the garden, went into her house, and shut the door. Mark gave Carol a kick. "You see, you've lost them both now," he said angrily. "She'll tell Grandma we quarreled and then Grandma

will say we can't have them. You always spoil everything, Carol."

"I didn't," sobbed Carol, kicking back as hard as she could. "They were my kittens and I found them. I hate you! I'm going to run away, so there! And I'll come back and get Fluff all by myself."

She was off, slamming the gate behind her and away she ran, down the hill. Mark couldn't see which way she went because the trees hid her from view.

4

Mark waited for a few minutes, just to show Carol that he didn't care if she did run away. Then he walked back to the shop and looked around. He couldn't see her any-where.

She was probably hiding, but he wished he knew. She might have run very fast and turned at the bend in the road that led to the cottage. She might now be telling tales to Grandma and Grandma would think it was all his fault, and of course it wasn't, not at all! He was the oldest, and the black and white kitten was by far the prettiest; and he wanted so badly to go and see the lighthouse. He sniffed and felt very sorry for himself.

On the other hand, she might have run

into the field opposite the shop and be hiding behind the barn. He was quite sure that she would not have run down the twisty little road that led to the sea because she was afraid of the dark woods. When they were not quarreling, he always held her hand when they ran between the trees. He didn't like them much himself.

He decided to search behind the barn, and if she wasn't there, he would go home and peek through the kitchen door to see if she had arrived first. If she was not there, he would pretend they were playing outside and wait until she turned up. Carol was such a baby. "Wait until I get her alone," he muttered. "I'll teach her! But not until after we've been to the lighthouse."

But Carol wasn't behind the barn, nor anywhere in the field, although he walked a little way along, peering into the hedge. He did not find her, but he found a hedge-sparrow's nest, beautifully woven from moss with five bright blue eggs in it. It was so beautiful that he almost forgot Carol and waited quite a long time, crouching in the grass, until the sparrow came back. Then he tiptoed away, feeling rather sorry. If only they had not quarreled, he could have shown Carol that nest. She would have loved it.

He thought he had better go home with the basket and see what was happening. Grandma would be wondering where he was, and if he was nice to Carol, they might still go to Hartland Point. He hurried up the road and stuck his nose cautiously around the back door.

It was very quiet in the kitchen. Grandma was all alone, doing the ironing. She looked up and smiled. "At last!" she said. "I thought you'd got lost and all my shopping with you. Where's Carol?"

"Oh . . . she's playing outside. Can we go

over to the farm for a bit?"

"Yes, for half an hour. We'll have lunch early and set off to the lighthouse."

Mark ran to the farm but Carol wasn't there. He was beginning to get very worried indeed. Whatever would Grandma say if she hadn't come back by lunchtime? And anyway, where was she? For the first time he started to feel really worried, not just about Grandma and the lighthouse, but about Carol herself.

He went back to the shop but the shopkeeper hadn't seen her. He stood at the top of the steep, winding road that led down to the sea and felt even more worried. But she couldn't have run down there all by herself; he was sure she couldn't. But half an hour was up and there was nothing to be done but to go back and tell Grandma. He shuffled into the kitchen.

"Come along," said Grandma, "lunch is all ready and I've made some nice biscuits for tea. Where's Carol?"

Mark hung his head. "I can't find her," he mumbled. "She ran away. I've looked everywhere for her."

"She ran away? But you said you were going to the farm. Did she run from the farm?"

"It was before that; she ran away from the shop. I've looked everywhere, honest I have."

"But you said she was playing outside. Just when did you lose her? Tell me at once, Mark. How long has she been gone?"

Mark burst into tears. He knew from her voice that Grandma was frightened and he suddenly felt very frightened too.

"I don't know," he sobbed. "She just ran. I couldn't see where she went. We were on the hill behind the shop and she ran behind the trees and when I came down she wasn't there."

"Well, if she hasn't come home and she isn't at the farm, she must have run down to the sea. It was very naughty of you, Mark, not to tell me sooner. We must drive down at once and look for her, and if she's not there, we must phone the police."

Grandma hurried to the garage and got out the car, calling to the neighbor to watch, in case Carol came back while they were

away. Mark jumped in beside her and they drove slowly down the road, looking to the left and right. Neither of them said anything at all. The road ended at the little cluster of white cottages and the shop that sold groceries, ice cream, cups of tea and blue china mugs. From there, the rocky footpath led down to the beach.

But there wasn't any beach. The tide had come in and the waves, blue and sparkling, were breaking against the cliff. Grandma turned and spoke to a man and his wife who were drinking tea at a table outside the shop.

"We've lost a little girl, eight years old," said Grandma. "Did you happen to notice a child by herself?"

The couple looked at each other.

"Why yes," said the woman, "about an hour ago when we came up from the beach. Don't you remember, John? A little girl ran past us; pretty little girl she was, with fair, curly hair. I thought her parents were down there. But she can't be there now. The tide's in."

"And you haven't seen her since?"

"Come to think of it, we haven't. But we were in the shop for a bit so maybe we didn't notice if she passed."

"Thank you." Grandma's voice sounded strange and tight. Mark glanced up at her and noticed that her face had turned quite white and she seemed to have forgotten all about him.

"I suppose she could have run along into the next cove," said Grandma. "The cliff is further back there and it may not be too late. We must call the Coast Guard at once."

She went back into the shop leaving Mark standing alone in the road that turned into a rocky path, staring out over the sea. Where, oh where was Carol?

5

Where was Carol?

When she ran away from the garden where the kittens lived, she was so angry that she hardly knew what she was doing. She wanted to run and run and give Mark a big scare. If she didn't come back for a long time, Grandma would be very upset with Mark for not looking after her, so she would run for a long way and get really, really lost.

She would run right down to the sea and hide behind the rocks. Mark would never catch up to her with that heavy basket. She was so angry that she hardly noticed the dark woods; she was much too busy thinking about that darling tabby kitten and hating Mark. "Fluff, Fluff," she cried to herself, "I wanted you so badly. If only I'd never shown Mark. If only I'd just gone in alone and got it. I won't come back, not for a long time. I hate him."

She ran right through the dark woods and came out into the sunshine, and the clumps of primroses on the banks were like great yellow pools. She stopped to smell them and noticed some white violets sheltering under a fern. She smelled them too, but she did not pick them, because she was not going home for a long, long time and they might die.

But she felt better out there in the sunshine, and by the time she had reached the cottages and looked down the path that led to the sea, she had almost decided to go home for lunch. But she still had plenty of time; she would hide for a little while in case Mark came to look for her.

She would not go down to the beach because the tide was quite high and all the people were coming up, but there was a little path that ran along the bottom of the cliff for quite a long way. It seemed to turn a corner

farther on and Mark would never think of looking for her there.

It was fun running along that path on that bright April morning. There were sea gulls nesting on the cliff and she watched the swoop of their white wings and almost forgot her troubles. She felt rather sorry. If only they hadn't quarreled, she could have shown Mark the gulls' nests. He would have loved them.

The path had turned a corner and she suddenly found herself in another little cove where the cliffs were much farther back. Here there was plenty of room and lots of sand and the water seemed quite far away. She had never been here before and she felt quite excited. She would bring Mark here as soon as they had made up from their quarrel. She thought it was even nicer than their own beach and she began to look for shells. There were little pools in the rocks too, with sea anemones waving their tendrils at her and tiny crabs scuttling to and fro. It was so warm and quiet and sheltered that she felt almost sleepy. She had no idea how late it was getting.

It was only when she happened to look up that she noticed how much nearer the water had come and she felt a little bit frightened. It must be nearly lunch time, she thought, and she still had to climb that steep hill home. She suddenly wanted to get back as quickly as possible. Mark had had plenty of time to have had a big, big scare and Grandma had had plenty of time to have been very upset with him. She began to wonder whether Grandma might not be rather upset with her too.

She ran to the place where the path had turned the corner and then she forgot all about Mark and Grandma and everything else and just stood staring and staring. For there ahead of her was nothing but water. The path was quite covered all the way to the bottom of the cliff and their beach wasn't there anymore. The tide had come in and there was nothing at all but sparkling blue water and little white waves breaking against the rocks.

Carol felt very frightened; she began to cry. She wondered if the sea would come right up to the cliffs in the new cove, because if so, she would be drowned. She couldn't get out either side. She tried to find a path up the cliff, but the rocks were too steep for a little girl to climb. She sat down on a big rock, and she had never felt so lonely and afraid before.

She knew that if she waited long enough, the tide would turn and the path would be there again, but she did not know how far the water would reach in the cove where she was sitting. It was getting nearer and nearer, quite close to her sandals. She thought of her mother and father and the new baby and the rabbits, but they were far away and they couldn't help her. She thought of Grandma and Mark. They would be out looking for her now, but how would they know where to look? She wanted Mark to come so badly; Mark would know what to do. She always felt safe when Mark was there. But how could he come when the path was covered with water?

Grandma and Mark; she began to think

about the cottage: the warm kitchen, the ap-
ple blossoms in the garden, and that cozy
time just before she went to sleep, when
Grandma sat on her bed telling stories and
Mark curled up under the blanket in his pajamas. She remembered the first story and
she began to think about it. It was about the
sea, not on a blue sparkly day like this, but
on a dark night and there were twelve men
who were very frightened, just like she was.
But Jesus had come walking on the water
and they hadn't been frightened anymore.
Everything was all right when Jesus came.

She remembered something else, too.
Grandma had said that Jesus was still here,
although we couldn't see him, and he loved
us and listened to us and wanted to help us.
Mark said he didn't believe it, but Grandma
had said it was true and Grandma knew
more than Mark. Suppose she told him that
she needed to be rescued and suppose he
came to her, walking on the water? She
didn't think he would; but at least she could
try.

"Jesus," she said, closing her eyes and

folding her hands because that was what Grandma did when she prayed, "please come and help me. Don't let the water come right to where I am. Please help me to get out."

She opened her eyes but she was still alone. She began to think about Jesus. Grandma had said that he was very good and he wanted us to be good too. But she had quarreled and kicked and been horrid to Mark. She shut her eyes again.

"Please help me," she said. "I won't quarrel anymore, ever, and if you like, I'll let Mark have the black and white kitten."

She opened her eyes again and blinked; a boat was coming very fast around the curve of the cliff. It was coming straight into the cove and she could hear the chug-chug of its engine. For a moment she thought it must be Jesus, but then she remembered that Jesus didn't come in motorboats, he walked on the water. Well, it didn't much matter who it was, as long as they were coming. She jumped up, ran to the edge of the water and shouted and waved with all her might.

The Coast Guard beached quite close to

her. He jumped out and lifted her into the boat. "Now, what's all this about?" he said, as he pushed off. "Scaring your Grandma and your brother out of their wits, you are. Don't you ever run off by yourself like that again!"

And Carol, holding tight to the side of the boat as it skimmed out of the cove, made up her mind that she never, never would.

6

Grandma and Mark sat on a big rock, just above the water line, waiting for the Coast Guard to come back. He had arrived very quickly after they had phoned him and he had agreed that it was quite possible that Carol had strayed into the next cove before the tide was right up. But he had said that cove would soon be covered as well and he'd better get going. He had started the engine and shot off around the corner.

Grandma did not speak at all. She seemed to have forgotten about Mark, sitting so quietly beside her, and he felt terribly lonely. He knew now that if anything bad had happened to Carol, it was all his fault. Perhaps Grandma was very angry with him and that was why she did not speak to him. He looked up at her and saw that her eyes were shut like when she prayed at night, and he knew that she was praying for Carol.

"I wonder if it does any good," thought Mark. He shut his eyes and began saying quietly to himself, "Please, God, if you're there, find Carol."

He started thinking about Carol. What if she never came back? It would be awful without Carol, and whatever would Mom and Dad say? He suddenly felt very sorry that he had kicked her and been selfish. "If Carol comes back," he said to himself, "I'll be really nice to her. I'll even let her have the tabby kitten."

Then he looked up and saw the boat swing around the curve in the coastline, much sooner than they had expected. Mark gave Grandma such a push that she nearly fell sideways off the rock. "Grandma," he yelled jumping up, "it's coming. Look! Can you see her?"

They stood together shading their eyes against the sun and suddenly Grandma gave a great sigh and sat down.

"She's there," she said. "Thank God!"

Mark rushed to the entrance of the little bay where the waves lapped against the wall. The Coast Guard drew in, waved cheerily to Grandma and hoisted Carol onto the steps. She and Mark stood with the water right over their sandals and hugged each other. Then Carol ran to Grandma. "Grandma," she said in a surprised voice, "why are you crying? Can't you see I'm safe?"

"Yes, I can," said Grandma, holding her tight. "That's why I'm crying." And then they all started laughing instead.

They were all rather quiet driving back up the hill. Mark and Carol knew that they had both been very naughty and if Grandma was going to be upset with them they really could not blame her. But Grandma was not upset with them. She just seemed very tired.

We've all had such an awful scare, thought Grandma. *We should all be happy now. Perhaps we will talk about it another time, or perhaps they have learned their lesson without any talking.*

It was too late to go to Hartland Point, so

they decided to go the next day. But they all enjoyed their lunch and when they had finished Carol was so tired that she fell asleep in the armchair. Then they went to the farm and fed the calves and both had a ride on the horse; and Mark did not say that Carol was too little. He helped her on and off and held the reins so that the horse would not trot too fast.

They went to bed tired but happy, and when Grandma came for the good-night story, both Mark and Carol felt that it would be a special sort of story and both listened hard. It was about ten men and they all had a terrible illness called leprosy.

"People still get it," said Mark. "In Africa."

"Yes," said Grandma, "but now it can be cured. There was no medicine for it then. They became covered with spots and sores and they had to leave their homes and towns so others wouldn't catch it. They had to live out on the hills and no one would go near them. Their families would leave food for them to pick up.

"But these ten men heard about Jesus

and they came and stood waiting for him on the hillside. They didn't dare come too near the road. When they saw Jesus coming they all started shouting at the tops of their voices, 'Jesus, master, have mercy on us.'

"Jesus stopped. He was not afraid of leprosy. He just wanted to help the men. He told them to go back to their homes because he knew that by the time they got there, they would all be well.

"And they believed him; they all started rushing down the road shouting for joy, and as they ran their illness was healed. Their spots and sores disappeared. They were going home strong and well.

"All except one! He suddenly stopped. He was a stranger from another country. Then he turned around and came running back to Jesus and fell down in front of him and began to thank him with all his heart.

"Jesus was rather sad. 'I healed ten,' he said. 'Where are the other nine? Has only one stopped to say thank you?,'

"But he was glad about the one. 'You can stand up and go in peace,' said Jesus. 'Your faith has made you well.'

"And the tenth man went home much happier than the others. The others had been healed, but the tenth had talked to Jesus and come to know him; and he had made Jesus glad by saying thank you."

"Will we say thank you because I was rescued?" asked Carol. "You know, Grandma, when I was there in that cove, I remembered about Jesus walking on the water and I asked him to help me, and then I saw the boat."

"It wasn't Jesus, it was the Coast Guard," said Mark.

"But that's how God answers our prayers," said Grandma. "Jesus isn't walking about on earth anymore, but his love and power are still here working through people. It was God who made those people outside the shop notice where you had gone, and who made the Coast Guard come so quickly. It was God who helped you to sit still and wait quietly instead of trying to climb the cliff or swim along the edge, or anything silly like that. We were praying and he was helping us all the time, and we must certainly thank him."

So they all shut their eyes and Grandma thanked God for looking after Carol and keeping her safe. Carol remembered that terrible moment when she knew that the water was all around her and Grandma and Mark remembered how they had sat on that rock and wondered if Carol had drowned. But it had all come out all right in the end. Even Mark knew that someone had been there, listening to them and helping them.

And Mark and Carol both remembered something else. Since coming home from the beach, no one had talked about the kittens at all. Those kittens needed an awful lot of thinking about.

7

The next morning, Mark found the sun pouring in through his bedroom window. It was a perfect day for Hartland Point and he jumped out of bed.

"Grandma," he shouted, "let's have breakfast soon and let's take a picnic to the lighthouse."

Grandma was in the kitchen in her robe, making herself a cup of tea, and she promised to get going early.

"I could go to the shop by myself this morning," said Mark, "and Carol could help you get ready. It would be quicker that way. And can we have potato chips and soda-pop with our picnic, Grandma?"

"Why yes," said Grandma, "and as a great

treat, we might finish up with cookies and milk at a farm near there. But Carol likes going to the shop, too, so we must wait and see what she wants.

To Grandma's surprise, Carol seemed quite pleased with the idea of Mark going shopping alone. In fact, she seemed in quite a hurry to get him out of the house, and as soon as he had left, she pulled Grandma down on the sofa beside her.

"Grandma," she said. "It's about those kittens."

"What kittens?" asked Grandma.

"The kittens we had a fight about," said Carol. "We didn't tell you, but that's why I ran away. They're in the house up the hill behind the shop and they're free; you don't have to pay anything, and I wanted the tabby—he's so sweet, Grandma, the sweetest little kitten you ever saw. But Mark wanted the black one and we had a big quarrel and I ran away, and then . . ."

Carol was suddenly quiet.

"Well?" said Grandma. "Go on."

"Well, when I was on the beach," said

Carol very slowly. "I just thought I didn't want to quarrel with Mark anymore, and I thought I'd let him have the black and white kitten after all. And Grandma, could we go and get it now, at once, and could we go across the field so we won't meet him? You see, I want it to be a surprise."

"But," said Grandma, "what will Mommy say? Does she want a kitten as well as a new baby?"

"She won't mind," said Carol. "There's lots of room for both at home. And if she really says we can't have it, you could keep it, Grandma, and we'd play with it when we come to stay."

"Well," said Grandma, "I wouldn't mind. I thought I heard a mouse in the storeroom the other day and I did think about getting a cat. Let's go at once, before Mark gets back."

They found a basket with a lid and went out through the back gate and crossed the field. It was a longer way but much prettier. The dew still lay on the grass, silver and shining, but the daisies and dandelions were beginning to open their faces to the sunshine.

Carol walked rather slowly and she did not say anything at all. It was going to be very hard to see that tabby kitten again and then leave it behind. As they came near to the cottage she took Grandma's hand and held it tight.

The woman who had showed them the kittens the day before had gone out, but her husband opened the door. He was pleased to see Grandma.

"Come for a kitten, have you?" he said. "The wife told me about your two young'uns yesterday. Made up your mind now, have you? We're in luck this morning. A lad came in not long ago and took one, just after the wife left for market . . ."

Carol gasped. Supposing someone had taken the black and white one, and she couldn't give Mark a surprise after all! She ran into the woodshed. It was all right; the black and white kitten was still there, clawing over the side of the basket. It was the tabby which had gone and Carol was glad. It would have been hard to see it and then to leave it behind.

She held Tippet in her arms. He was very soft and fluffy and looked up at her with big, baby blue eyes. She stroked him softly. "Dear, dear little Tippet," she whispered. "You are not quite as nice as Fluff but I love you very much." Then she took Grandma's hand. "Grandma, let's go now," she said. "I want to show Mark. He'll be home by now."

They hurried home up the road, carrying the kitten hidden in the basket. When they reached the cottage, Mark was hanging over the gate, looking very pleased with himself.

"Where have you been?" he said. "I've been looking everywhere for you. You'd better come into the kitchen 'cause I've got a surprise for you."

"So have I for you," shouted Carol. She rushed into the kitchen and there, in the middle of the table, was the tabby kitten lapping milk out of Grandma's best china saucer.

"It's Fluff," screamed Carol, "and here's Tippet." She opened the basket and Tippet leaped out and tried to push Fluff away from the milk. They both jumped into the saucer

and the milk went all over the tablecloth. The kittens stuck their tails in the air and lapped it up.

"For goodness sake, put them on the floor," said Grandma who thought for a moment that she was seeing double. "And get that cloth in to soak. And they can't drink out of my best tea saucer either. Look, there's a tin plate over on the sink and until they are house-trained, they must sleep in the shed. I don't know what Mommy is going to say about it all. We'll phone her tonight."

"Can we take the kittens on the picnic?" said Mark.

"We couldn't leave them behind," said Carol.

So when they had made the sandwiches and packed the picnic and the bathing things, they all set off; Grandma driving in front and Mark, Carol, Tippet and Fluff at the back. The kittens traveled in a big cardboard box lined with an old wool sweater of Grandma's. They snuggled down and looked very warm and comfortable and when they reached the lighthouse and had lunch, they ran about in the daisies. In the afternoon, they went on to a little beach and Mark and Carol swam. Grandma sat on a rock and the kittens rolled in the sand. They all finished with milk and cookies at a farm; it was a beautiful day.

And all the time Mark felt loving to Carol because she had given him Tippet and Carol felt loving to Mark because he had given her Fluff. And because they were loving, they were happy; and that was why it was such a beautiful day.

8

They phoned Mom that evening at six o'clock. Grandma spoke first and Mark and Carol jumped up and down in the doorway. Of course they could only hear what was being said at one end of the phone, but they more or less knew what was happening by listening to Grandma.

"How are things going, dear?" asked Grandma. "Not long? . . . Good . . . Oh, they're fine but they wanted me to ask you something. Would you mind if they each brought home a kitten? . . . Well yes, I know and I'm sorry, but it was a mistake; they each got one for the other . . . Yes, it was meant to be only one; it was all a mistake. I'll write and explain . . . No, there won't be lots more; they are both males. Yes dear, I do realize there's going to be a baby, but it would be safer on the veranda; there are other cats besides these . . . Yes, I know it's all an extra expense but I'll contribute to the cat food . . . Well, just think it over dear, and let us know . . . I'll pass you over to Mark."

Mark took the receiver and Carol listened anxiously.

"Mom, it will be all right about the baby," he said, very fast and loud. "I had a friend at school and they had a baby and a stroller and a cat and they put a net over it . . . No, Mom, not over the cat, over the stroller . . . It would be much safer because the Browns next door have a huge cat. Okay, Mom, ask Dad and tell us tomorrow, but please say yes . . ."

Carol snatched the receiver from him. "Mom," she squealed, "they're the sweetest little kittens you ever saw, their names are Fluff and Tippet. And Mom, there was only going to be one but we quarreled, and I ran away and the tide came up and I was nearly drowned, and the Coast Guard rescued me and then we both went and got the other one

by mistake . . . No Mommy, it's all right, I didn't drown at all. I'm quite all right . . . I was just telling you . . ."

Grandma took the receiver firmly from Carol.

"Carol's fine," she said, "and I'll write and tell you all about it. Just let us know at once if the baby comes. Bye now and God bless. We'll phone tomorrow at six."

But they didn't phone at six because Dad phoned them at five, and it wasn't about kittens. When they heard the phone ring Mark and Carol went on eating their snack because they thought it was too early for a call from home. Only when they heard what Grandma was saying did they run out into the hallway and start to clap softly.

"A little boy!" cried Grandma. "Oh, Brian, I'm so very thankful . . . after Grandpa? How lovely! . . . Is Anne all right? . . . Splendid . . . Yes, I'll have them all ready by lunchtime. They'll be wild to get home. Here they are."

"It's a boy," whispered Mark. "Hurrah!"

"It's a baby," thought Carol, "and I don't care if it's a boy or a girl. Mom said I could bathe it and take it out in the stroller."

Dad told them both, all over again, about Richard John, named after Grandpa, who weighed nine pounds, three ounces and had lots of dark hair and a very loud voice, and when Dad had finished, Carol said, "And what about the kittens? Can we have them?"

"Kittens?" said Dad. "What kittens?"

"Our kittens, Fluff and Tippet. Did Mom forget to tell you?"

"Well, she was rather busy thinking about the baby last night. What about them?"

"Well, can we have them? One each."

"Oh sure, if you'll look after them. A couple of kittens shouldn't be too much trouble. Have them ready in a box when I come on Friday."

"Friday!" cried Carol, jumping up and down. "That's the day after tomorrow. Couldn't we go tomorrow, Grandma? I just can't wait to see the baby."

Mark looked thoughtful. He went to Grandma and rubbed his head against her shoulder. "It's not that we want to leave you, Grandma," he said. "We've had a really good time. It's just that we're anxious to see the baby. Couldn't you come with us?"

Grandma rumpled his hair. "It's all right, Mark," she said. "I understand. I'm anxious to see the baby too, but Auntie's quite close and she'll give a hand. I was hoping you might all come and stay for your summer vacation. That's less than three months away."

The children thought that this was a lovely plan, and after all, the time went quickly. They went into Bideford the next morning and bought presents for the baby with their pocket money, a bib with a robin on it and a pink rattle with a bell inside. In the afternoon, they had a last swim, and then it was time to pick primroses for Mom, say goodbye to the farmer and the animals, to pack, and watch the kittens have their supper. Then at last Carol was safe in bed and Mark was sitting crosslegged at the other end with the blanket around him. Grandma leaned back in the armchair. She looked quite tired.

"Tomorrow," said Carol, wriggling her toes, "I will be holding the baby."

"And me," said Mark. "You've got to take turns."

"He's a very lucky baby," said Grandma quickly, before an argument could start, "to be born into a family like yours, with a loving mother and father, a sister old enough to look after him and a brother old enough to teach him and protect him."

"And two kittens," said Carol.

"And four rabbits," said Mark.

"And all our toys," said Carol. "Oh, I just can't wait! Grandma, tell us a story, a special one because it's our last night."

"Very well," said Grandma. "We've been talking about the baby born into your family, so I'll tell you about a man who wanted to be born again."

"How silly," said Mark.

"You couldn't," said Carol.

"Wait and see," said Grandma.

She told them how the religious leaders of the country where Jesus lived became very jealous of Jesus. Jesus was healing sick people and making the blind see and of course everyone loved him and followed him, and no one listened to the ordinary teachers at all. Everyone wanted Jesus.

So the leaders and teachers got together and they made a plan. They told the people that Jesus was a wicked man and they must not go to him or listen to him. But one leader, called Nicodemus, wanted to listen. He knew that Jesus was good and loving but he was afraid to be seen visiting him. So he waited until it was quite dark and then he crept along the streets and knocked at the door.

"Come in," said Jesus.

"Master," said Nicodemus, "I know that God has sent you, and I want to know how you do all these wonderful things."

Jesus said to him, "If you want to under-stand, you must be born again."

"That's silly," said Mark. "I said so before."

"What did he mean?" said Carol.

"That's just what Nicodemus wanted to know," said Grandma. "He was like Mark. We've been talking about your baby, born into your family, belonging to Mom and Dad. Jesus is God's Son and when we come to him and love him, then we become God's children too, and God becomes our heavenly Father. We are born into God's family and all the other people who love Jesus are like our brothers and sisters and we all love and help each other."

"How?" asked Carol.

"Just by asking," said Grandma. "Tell God you want to belong to him and call him your heavenly Father. Tell him you want to live his way and love like Jesus loved. Then he will make you part of his family."

They talked for a little longer and Grandma prayed. She thanked God for the new baby and asked that Mark and Carol would understand what it meant to be born into God's family. Then she tucked Carol in and kissed them both good-night. "Go to sleep quickly," she said, "and then it will be tomorrow."

Mark went to his room. He knelt at his window with his arms on the sill, and looked out at the black Bristol Channel and the great dark sky above it, with stars shining millions of miles away. It was so big and wide that it made him feel rather small and lonely.

Perhaps it would be good to know that he belonged to a heavenly Father who guided the stars and the sea, but who still cared about one boy.

Carol snuggled down under the blankets and thought about the baby, *Our family . . . God's family . . . Mom and Dad, Mark and me and Richard John . . . Fluff, Tippet and the rabbits, and a loving heavenly Father . . . it's nice to belong. . . .*

And Carol was asleep.